The

REAL
FAIRY
Storybook

Georgie Adams

illustrated by
Sally Gardner

Dolphin

For Giselle
- a dear friend and very good fairy!
With love from G.A.

For Georgie
With love from S.G.

Published in paperback in 1999
First published in Great Britain in 1998
by Orion Children's Books
a division of the Orion Publishing Group Ltd
Orion House
5 Upper Saint Martin's Lane
London WC2H 9EA

A catalogue record for this book is available from the British Library

Printed in Italy by Printer Trento Srl

Contents

Hello. Who are you?
Nicole

Goodness you made us jump,

popping in like that.

Nightwing

Blossom

How clever of you to find us. Now don't run
away — we won't bite! Come and sit down.
Come along, over here, but mind you don't tread
on the dress. That would never do!

Tell me your name again, I have forgotten it
already. I am rather forgetful, I'm afraid. What
was that? Oh, yes. My name is Blossom
— Royal Dressmaker, if you please —
and these are my assistants,
Nightwing, Fancy, Trip and . .
Pod. Pod! Pod! Where are
you? Come out from under
that pile of pearls and meet. .

Trip

Fancy

There I go again! Your name has gone in one ear and out of the other. Go on, introduce yourself. Pod is rather shy, and a little overwhelmed at meeting you, but she'll be fine in a tick or two.

. . tick, tick, tick, that reminds me, time is flying by and we have to finish this dress by midnight.

Pod

Who is it for? The Fairy Queen, of course! She's to wear it to the Midsummer Ball, though goodness knows how we'll sew on all these pearls in time. It's seven o'clock now. How many pearls, did you ask? How many? **ONE THOUSAND** pearls, that's how many! And each one has to be stitched with gossamer thread, as fine as fine.

9

Bother! Now I've dropped my needle. It will be running off with the thimble, before you can blink — up to all tricks and stitches, I shouldn't wonder. Could you help me find it? It can't be far away.

And while you're looking, I'll tell you a story. It will help to pass the time. Would you like that? Good. Then I'll begin . . .

THE SEAHORSE AND THE KELPIE KING

ONCE UPON A TIME, THERE WAS A LITTLE SEAHORSE. He bobbed about in the waves that splashed along the shore and sometimes he would be tossed into a rock pool, where the water-fairies played. Then they had such fun together playing hide and seek. The little seahorse often let the fairies ride on his back.

I suppose life for the little seahorse might have gone on happily in this way, but one dark night there was a terrible storm.

Thunder boomed overhead and streaks of lightning flashed across the sky.

The little seahorse was terrified! He swam far away from home until, by ill fortune, he reached the deep and murky waters where the kelpies lived. And, if you did not already know, let me tell you that kelpies are ugly, bad sprites all good fairies fear.

The sea was very rough. Huge waves swept the little seahorse high into the air, and dropped him down into a foaming whirlpool. As he was swirling round, he felt something grab his tail. He had been caught by a kelpie!

"Got you!" screeched the horrible creature.

"You'll make a tasty meal for the King."

The little seahorse struggled to free himself from the slimy claw but the kelpie held on tight, and swam with his catch to the bottom of the sea.

It was a different world down there, unlike anything the little seahorse had ever known.

The kelpie took him through a forest of strange plants, as big as trees, that led to an enormous cave. Inside, on a rocky throne surrounded by fat sea snails, sat the Kelpie King – the biggest and ugliest kelpie of them all. He grinned at the little seahorse, and his breath smelt of rotting bones.

"Lock him up," said the king.
"I'll eat him for supper."

Before the little seahorse knew what was happening, the kelpie threw him into a giant clam, and slammed the shell shut. Oh! thought the little seahorse, all alone in the dark, this is the end of me. And he wished and *wished* he could be at home with the fairies by the shore . . .

Now it so happened that the water-fairies knew all about the little seahorse and his troubles. Fairies have a way of knowing about such things, and they were already flying to help him. They were brave, I can tell you! All fairies are afraid of those bad kelpies, and quite powerless against them. Still, the little seahorse was their friend and they wanted to save him if they could. In no time the fairies found that dreadful cave, and hid behind the clam.

At supper time that evening the Kelpie King took the little seahorse, and opened his mouth wide . . .

"Please, *please*, don't eat him!" cried the fairies, swimming out from their hiding place. Please spare him."

The King looked surprised to see the water-fairies; none had ever dared come near him before. Then he peered at the little seahorse with one bulgy eye. He thought he was a *very small* morsel, and hardly worth bothering about. But he was much too mean to let the little seahorse go. Instead he thought of a way to amuse himself. He turned to the fairies, saying,

"I'll spare your friend tonight. But you must bring me a lock of hair from a mermaid by sunrise, or

I'LL EAT HIM UP!"

The little seahorse trembled as the king ordered him to be locked in the clam again. But before it slammed shut, the fairies whispered in his ear,

"Leave this to us. We'll soon set you free. We'll be back before dawn, with the hair. Wait and see!"

Sure enough next morning, just as the sun was rising, the water-fairies returned with the mermaid's hair. When they gave it to the king, he was furious. He was sure he had set them a task they couldn't do. So he kept the little seahorse prisoner for a second day. The fairies thought this was most unfair, but they stayed close by the clam.

Again at supper time that evening the Kelpie King took the little seahorse, and opened his mouth wide. The little seahorse was terrified, and shook from his nose to his tail.

19

"Please, *please*, don't eat him!" cried the fairies.

The King thought for a moment and said, "I'll spare your friend tonight, but you must bring me the shadow of a child by sunrise, or

I'LL EAT HIM UP!"

The King thought this was an impossible task for the fairies, and the seahorse thought so too. Tears rolled down his nose as he was put in the clam again. But before it slammed shut, the fairies whispered in his ear,

"Leave this to us. We'll soon set you free. We'll be back before dawn with the shadow, you'll see!"

This time the fairies flew up into the dark night sky. The moon was shining on the world below, and they could see everything clearly. Soon they spotted the very thing they were looking for. They folded their wings

and slid down a moonbeam into . . .

a beautiful garden. There they found a statue of a child, with the moonlight casting a shadow.

21

Quick as winks the fairies rolled up the shadow, and tied it in a neat little parcel with cobweb strings. Then they flew as fast as they could out of the garden and down to the sea. The sun was just rising as they dived into the waves to the kelpies' cave below.

Well, the Kelpie King jumped up and down with rage when the fairies gave him the child's shadow (only a bit crumpled for being squashed in a parcel). He was sure he had given them a task they couldn't do. So he kept the little seahorse prisoner for a third day, and the fairies remained close by.

Again at supper that evening, the king took the little seahorse, and opened his mouth wide.

"Please, *please,* don't eat him," cried the fairies, for the third time. "We'll do anything you ask, if you'll spare him."

A wicked smile spread over the Kelpie King's face. He had thought of something this time he was sure the fairies could not do.

"I'll spare your friend tonight," he said. "But you must bring me all the colours of the rainbow by sunrise. If you can do this, then I'll let the seahorse go."

The little seahorse was at his wits' end, as a kelpie threw him into the clam again. But before it slammed shut the fairies whispered in his ear,

"Leave this to us. We'll soon set you free. We'll be back before dawn with a rainbow, you'll see!"

Straightaway the fairies flew to their Fairy Queen, who lived by the shore. Only they knew she possessed a necklace of jewels cut from a rainbow. Each jewel sparkled with dazzling colours.

When the fairies told the queen about the little seahorse, she gave them the necklace at once.

"Here," she said, "take this to that wicked kelpie. You may be sure he'll be sorry he ever asked for such a thing!"

Then the fairies flew with the precious necklace, over the sea, and down into the dark depths of the kelpies' cave. As the sun was rising they gave the necklace to the Kelpie King. Each jewel sparkled with rainbow colours, like a comet showering stars.

The king snatched the necklace angrily. Oh, then how he howled with rage! Each brilliant jewel burned his fingers like red hot coals, hissing and steaming in the bubbling sea. No matter how hard the kelpie tried to shake himself free, the burning necklace stuck fast.

"Only the coldest icebergs of the north can melt those fiery jewels," said the fairies. "We have done all you asked. Now set the little seahorse free."

At once the clam sprang open and out swam the little seahorse, as happy as he could be to see the clever fairies. The Kelpie King made off, yelping and howling all the way to the icy north, and was never seen or heard of again.

And as far as I know, the little seahorse still lives by the shore . . . and fairies often ride on his back!

Did you like that story?
Do nod if you did. Is it true,
you ask? Is it true?
Of course it is!

Every word of it. That's because it's a **REAL** fairy story, you see. Not like some you hear these days. And there are others. You will stay and listen, won't you? We love telling stories and . . .

OUCH! There now, I have found that needle, and pricked my finger. Quick, Trip, bind my finger, before I make more mess. I shall have to stitch petal patches over these splodges, as it is.

Dear me, just look at the time! We still have **EIGHT HUNDRED** pearls to sew before midnight. And there's the hem to finish . . .

Nightwing, are you sure the hem is straight? It looks crooked to me. Up one side, and dipperty down the other - all higgledy-piggledy. You had better start again. Fancy, stop laughing and help Nightwing with the pins and tape measure.

Now, do you see a button box anywhere about? We shall need buttons to fasten at the back. Twelve little round red buttons would do it. Could you help us find them? Thank you. I don't know what we should do without you.

And while you're busy with the buttons, Pod will tell us a story. Come along, Pod, don't be shy. You know such funny stories. Think of one now. We're all listening . . .

When I Was a Tooth Fairy

WELL, I COULD TELL YOU ABOUT THE TIME I WAS A TOOTH FAIRY. It was my first job; I wasn't very good at it, and one night I made a terrible mistake. It all began like this . . .

I had just curled up in my bed. My pillow was full of dreams, and I was settling down for a good night's sleep when, *Clang! Clang! Clang!* The Tooth Bell rang. There is no knowing when a tooth will fall out, and when a tooth fairy will have to collect it.

29

Children spend a lot of time wiggling their teeth to make them loose. A difficult tooth will hang on by a thread for ages. Then, when the owner is least expecting it, *pop!* Out it comes. That is what happened to a boy called Patrick.

Patrick had been tugging away at his tooth all day. It was a front tooth (they are the worst) and it wouldn't let go – even though it was very wobbly. But while Patrick was chewing a toffee . . . *oooof!* It fell out. And there it was – a little sticky, but a good tooth just the same.

It may surprise you to learn that some people (mostly grown-ups) do not believe in fairies. It is hurtful, but there it is. Curiously, children who say they don't believe in them suddenly change their minds as soon as a tooth falls out. It was like that with Patrick.

"Will the fairies give me lots of money for my tooth?" he asked his mother at bedtime.

"I didn't think you believed in all that stuff," she said.

"Er . . . I do, " said Patrick, not very convincingly. "So, how much do you think it's worth?"

"Not much, all stuck up with toffee," said his mother.

So, Patrick brushed his tooth until it sparkled. Then he put it under his pillow, and fell asleep. Which is when the Tooth Bell rang, and I flew off to find him.

Patrick lived at Number Sixty-Two, Sky View Flats in the middle of a big city. Fairies find cities very confusing, so it took me a while to find his address. And once inside Sky View Flats, I discovered it had many floors. On each one, there were lots of doors with numbers.

Now I should explain that I have never been very good with numbers. I could grant you THREE wishes without any trouble. I know how many beans make FIVE. After that I get in a muddle.

That night I flew along one long corridor after another looking at all the numbers, and getting more and more muddled. Eventually I stopped outside Number Twenty-Six. It looked the right number to me, so I slipped through the keyhole. In two blinks, I was sure I had found Patrick's bedroom. The boy (or so I thought) was huddled under the bedclothes, and on the bedside table were some teeth. Not just one tooth, but A WHOLE SET of them, floating in a glass of water.

A more experienced fairy would have known something was not quite right. But you must remember that I was very new to the job, and it was exciting to find so many teeth all at once. I took the teeth and in return left behind a large bag of silver. I thought that was a fair exchange.

33

But later, when I showed the Chief Tooth
Fairy what I had brought, she was very cross.

"You silly fairy!" she cried. "They're false.
False! We can't make pearls from FALSE
TEETH! Only the whitest, pearliest baby teeth
will do. *That's* what fairy pearls are made of."

So I lost my job.

That same night another fairy went
to Number Sixty-Two to collect
Patrick's real tooth. The next
morning he found a silver
coin under his pillow, and
was very pleased.

As for the owner of the teeth at Number *Twenty-Six* . . . it turned out that they belonged to an old man called Harold. When he woke up the next morning, he was amazed to find a bag of silver in place of his false teeth (which had never fitted him properly anyway). And he has believed in fairies ever since!

What a story, Pod! I'm sure I should have made the same mistake myself.

And all that talk of teeth and toffees has made me peckish. So I think we should stop for a bite to eat. We can make time for a snack. Fancy, blow the clock back a tick or two.

What is there to eat, you ask? Anything you wish! You are in Fairyland, remember? Go on. Wish for something nice.

Oh, good. Here come the fairy cakes (I wished for those myself). Would you like to try one? Of course you would. They are simply delicious. Jump up and grab one as it goes past. The pink ones fly

very fast – they're quite a job
to catch – but the green ones
are slower . . .

Ooops! silly me, now I've dropped some jam on
the dress. Never mind, I'll dab it off
later. Mmm! I just
can't resist another
fairy cake, though I'm
quite out of puff from
catching the last one.
Then we must brush the
crumbs away and get back to work.

We still have so many pearls to stitch. How
many more, do you think? SIX HUNDRED I
should guess. Which gives us plenty of time for
more stories. Fancy, it's your turn, I think.
Tell us a story while we sew . . .

PRINCESS CURLY LONG LOCKS

ONCE UPON A TIME THERE LIVED A KING AND QUEEN, WHO WISHED MORE THAN ANYTHING FOR A BABY. Many years passed before their wish came true, but at last they had a daughter. They called her Curly Long Locks, and thought she was the loveliest child in the world.

Because she was their only child, the king and queen gave her everything she wanted, and the young princess grew up to be very spoilt. She bossed the palace servants about quite dreadfully, and never said 'please' or 'thank you'. Once she marched into the palace kitchen while Cook was cooking lunch.

"Bake me a cake," ordered Curly Long Locks.

"I'll make you one for tea," said Cook, busily rolling out pastry.

"No," said the princess. "I want one NOW!"

So Cook had to stop what she was doing and make a cake.

When lunch was a little late that day Cook got into trouble, which wasn't fair.

It was the same with her friends. Whenever children came to play at the palace, Curly Long Locks chose all the games and ordered everyone about. So her friends stopped coming.

One day while Curly Long Locks was in the garden, she saw a little boy staring at her through the palace gates. His name was Jack. He felt sorry for the princess playing on her own. He had no mother or father, brothers or sisters, and knew what it was like to be lonely. But Curly Long Locks turned her nose up in the air, and didn't even say, "Hello."

The best thing about Curly Long Locks was her shiny auburn hair; the reddish-brown strands were as bright as autumn leaves. Every day the nursemaids tried to brush the royal ringlets, but every day the princess made a fuss. And all because Her Royal Highness DID NOT LIKE HAVING HER HAIR DONE. You never heard such a noise! She screamed the place down, and kicked her poor nursemaids black and blue.

At hair-brushing time the queen tried everything to please her precious tot. She bought Curly Long Locks the prettiest dresses, the daintiest shoes, and chocolates to make your mouth water. But nothing worked. The princess wriggled, squirmed and stamped her foot. You see what a temper she had?

One morning while the nursemaids were
doing their best to plait the royal braids, the
queen brought Curly Long Locks a beautiful
doll. The princess was yelling at the top of her
voice, as usual. She grabbed the doll and threw
it out of the window.

An old woman happened to be walking by
the palace just then, and the doll landed at
her feet. The old woman (who was really a
fairy in disguise) stooped to pick it up.

"Give me back my doll!" shouted Curly
Long Locks from the open window.

"First, you must promise to be good," said the fairy.

"I won't! I WON'T!" yelled the princess.

"Very well, I shall keep the doll, and put YOU under a spell," said the fairy.

Curly Long Locks was about to say something rude to the old woman when the fairy changed her shape. The princess looked alarmed. She could see this *was* a real fairy, with wings and a wand. The princess was about to ask the fairy what sort of a spell she had cast when, as fairies often do, she vanished.

At first Curly Long Locks pretended not to care.

"Silly old fairy," she said to herself. "I bet she can't do magic."

At breakfast time she didn't *feel* any different. At lunch time she didn't *look* any different. But at teatime, while the princess was tucking into a plateful of cream buns . . .

her hair began to grow. In no time long, thick, curly locks had grown all around her face. It made eating sticky buns quite difficult.

Curly Long Locks' hair grew faster and faster. The king and queen stared in astonishment as their daughter's hair grew longer by the minute -

down to her waist,

past her knees,

over her feet and . . .

onto the floor.

Curly Long Locks was hopping mad! And hopping was all she *could* do, because by now the hair had wound itself around her ankles. The unfortunate princess could hardly put one foot in front of the other without tripping over.

"DO SOMETHING!" shouted Curly Long Locks angrily.

Soon news of the princess's plight spread throughout the palace. The nursemaids came running to the tea room, followed by the Lord Chancellor, three gardeners, a coachman and the cook. They had a job not to tread on the princess's hair, because it had spread over the floor like a carpet. Her curls were climbing up the walls and round the door.

Now Curly Long Locks was beginning to feel very much afraid. The princess was sorry she had been so rude to the fairy, and told everyone what had happened.

The queen frowned and scolded Cook, who was giggling in a corner with the coachman. The king straightened his crown, and asked the Lord Chancellor for his advice.

"Well," said the Lord Chancellor, trying not to laugh, "if Her Royal Highness is under some sort of spell, there's no knowing how long it could last - a day, a week, a year . . . maybe more. Who can tell?"

The king and queen were horrified.

All this time the hair had been growing thicker and longer. First the nursemaids tried to gather it up and tie it in bunches. It was like working in a hayfield! The hairbands kept snapping, and soon they ran out of ribbons.

Then the gardeners fetched rakes and shears and did their best to tidy things up. But the hair kept on growing.

That evening Curly Long Locks went to bed feeling miserable. The queen and all her ladies-in-waiting tried to comfort the unhappy child. They read bedtime stories and sang soothing lullabies, but they couldn't stop her crying. Her hair was as hot and heavy as a hundred eiderdowns.

And all through the night it grew and grew, until the whole palace was covered in hair.

In the morning the king summoned the Lord Chancellor to An Important Meeting. Something had to be done.

"Her Royal Highness must have her hair cut at once," said the king.

"But we've only got one pair of scissors," said the Lord Chancellor, "and they're not very sharp."

"Then send for the army!" ordered the king. "We must find all the scissors in the kingdom."

So that was arranged. Soldiers went out to every town and village in the land. Anyone with a pair of scissors had to go and cut the princess's hair. Tailors, barbers and dressmakers hurried to help; farmers with sickles and scythes came too. By the time they reached the palace, the hair was creeping over the walls, and along the road.

Snip, snip, snap! went the scissors.

Clip, clip, clip! went the shears.

Swish, swish, swish! went the scythes.

Curly Long Locks watched mournfully from the palace tower. Everyone clipped, snipped and trimmed from early morning till late at night. It kept the scissor-sharpeners busy. But no matter how much was cut, the princess's hair grew more vigorously than ever.

Days passed - then weeks, and months. The princess looked pale and thin. Her hair had grown so heavy, she could hardly eat or move. By the time a year had passed,

THE WHOLE KINGDOM WAS COVERED IN HAIR.

On the morning of Curly Long Locks' sixth birthday Jack was passing some shops on his way to the palace. Ever since the day he had seen the princess in the garden, he had thought of her. And, of course, he had heard about the fairy's spell. Jack felt very sorry for Curly Long Locks; he wanted to buy her a birthday present, but he knew the two small coins in his pocket wouldn't go far.

He stopped outside one shop, and pressed his nose to the window. The shop was full of old things, all jumbled up together. Right in the middle sat the most beautiful doll. Jack gazed at the doll. The doll seemed to smile at him. Then the old woman who owned the shop beckoned for Jack to come inside.

"Please," said Jack, "how much is that doll?"

"How much are you willing to pay?" asked the old woman, eyeing Jack in his thin, raggedy clothes.

"I have two small coins," replied Jack.

"Done!" said the old woman, and gave the boy the doll.

Jack couldn't believe his luck. He ran straight to the palace. The gates were hidden behind a thick bush of reddish-brown curls, so he climbed a plait and jumped over the wall.

A palace guard spotted him straightaway.

"Stop!" ordered the guard. "You can't come in here."

"Oh, *please!*" said Jack. "Look, I have brought the princess a birthday present. I really would like to give it to her myself."

The guard looked at Jack and the doll. He thought the princess would be pleased to see *somebody* on her birthday - even a scruffy lad like this.

"Very well," said the guard, "follow me."

The guard marched Jack down long corridors, and up some marble stairs to the princess's playroom. They had a job finding the door because it was covered in hair.

"In you go," said the guard. And he added, "Good luck!"

Jack knocked at the door and went in. The princess peered at Jack through a tangled mass of hair. There was something familiar about the boy's dirty face, but she couldn't think what.

"Who are you?" she said.

"I'm Jack," said Jack. Then, because he was a bit nervous and shy, he said all in a rush, "I saw you once when I was outside the palace gates and you were in the garden and I said Hello but you didn't hear and now I've brought you a present . . . Happy Birthday!"

Jack gave Curly Long Locks the doll. The princess took it . . . and gasped. Was it? How could it be? Yes! She was sure it was the *same* doll the queen had given her.

"I bought it off an old woman," explained Jack. "I hope you like it?"

Curly Long Locks nodded - a little stiffly because her hair was so heavy. Then, to her utter amazement, the doll nodded too. Jack and the princess looked more closely. Now the doll was grinning at them, and winking an eye! And slowly, ever so slowly, the doll changed shape until it had turned into a fairy. It was the fairy who had cast the spell! Jack could scarcely believe his eyes. He had never seen a fairy before. But the princess recognised her at once.

"Dear me," said the fairy, settling herself on a pile of curls. "Things are in a mess."

"Well, take your horrid spell away," said the princess.

"Say *please*," said the fairy.

"PLEASE!" said the princess quickly.

"That's better," said the fairy. "But to break my spell, you must wish for something that will make someone happy."

Curly Long Locks had never thought about anyone except herself, but she didn't have to think for long. She looked at Jack. He had been very kind. After all, it was Jack who had found the special doll. If all that hadn't happened, who knows? The spell might have lasted for ever!

"I *wish* . . . Jack could live with me at the palace," she said.

Jack couldn't have wished for anything better. So the spell was broken and the princess's hair stopped growing. After that Jack came to live at the palace. He became Prince Jack and the king and queen loved him as if he were their own son. Curly Long Locks grew to be much nicer. She brushed her hair every day, and always said 'please' and 'thank you'!

As for the fairy . . . she was never seen again, although the doll she left behind looked strangely like her.

Some peculiar things happened while you were telling that story, Fancy.

First the sleeves puffed themselves up like balloons, quite out of control. Then those little buttons I had ready to use suddenly turned into frogs. And every one of them has hopped off, to goodness knows where.

By the way, has anyone seen my wand? I'm sure I left it by the button box. Come to think of it, I saw Thimble and Thread near it a while ago ... I have a suspicion they may know something about a missing wand. Can you see them anywhere about? We must find them before they get up to any more mischief, or this dress will be ruined.

Does the dress fit, did you ask? Does it fit? Now, there's a good question. Does anyone know the answer? I'm afraid not. Perhaps one of us should try it on?

Nightwing . . . no, you are too tall.

Pod? A little short, maybe.

Trip or Fancy? Both too slim, I think.

That leaves me, Blossom. The Queen and I do have the same, er, shapely figures. Wait a tick while I slip it on. Then I'll twirl to give you a good all-round view.

There! How do I look? The bodice does feel a *little* tight after all those fairy cakes . . . but I think it will do.

Oh my poppers and pins, just look at the time! It's gone ten tocks, and we have another **FOUR HUNDRED** pearls to stitch before midnight. And, since a good fairy tale always helps to get the work done, let's have another.

Whose turn is it for a story? Trip, will you tell us one? We're all ready, so do begin . . .

THE SHOEMAKER
AND THE ROBBER ELVES

ONCE UPON A TIME THERE WAS A SHOEMAKER CALLED MR BOOT, WHO MADE THE BEST SHOES IN TOWN.

People came from miles around to Mr Boot's shoe shop - customers with

flat feet,
fat feet,
every this and that feet -

there wasn't a foot he couldn't fit!

Every day Mr Boot opened his shop in the High Street and people came bustling in. They bought slippers, sandals, boots and shoes - everything from clogs to dancing pumps. Mr Boot made them all.

In the evenings, when the shop was closed, Mr Boot made new shoes. He cut out the leather, stitched the soles and nailed the heels with his hammer. Then he polished the boots, laced up the shoes, and put them in the window, ready for his customers in the morning. You see how hard he worked! Mr Boot never went to bed before eleven o'clock.

One night while Mr Boot was fast asleep
upstairs in his bedroom, two elves called
Oddkin and Bodkin came creeping into his
shop. They were robbers! They looked at all
the shiny shoes and grinned.

"We can sell these at market," said Oddkin.

"The fairies will pay a good price for them,"
said Bodkin.

Of course, the shoes were much too big for
little folk so the elves chanted some magic
words, to make them smaller:

Shoes in twos, so fine and neat
SHRINK to fit wee fairy feet!

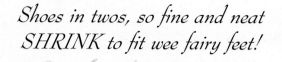

All the shoes shrank, to the
weeniest size imaginable. Then
the robber elves bundled their
booty in a sack, and were gone.

The next morning when Mr Boot opened his
shop, he couldn't believe his eyes. There wasn't
a shoe left on the shelf!

"I've been robbed!" he cried.

The shoemaker was hopping and skipping
mad. He had nothing to sell, and his
customers were none too pleased about it.

"I'll make some more shoes today," promised
Mr Boot. "Please come back tomorrow."

So everyone huffed and
puffed, and went off
grumbling.

Mr Boot cobbled furiously all that day, and late into the evening. He cut, hammered, stitched and trimmed, faster than he had ever worked before. His fingers were sore and his eyes ached but at last he had a stock of new shoes to sell. It was nearly midnight before he switched off the light and went to bed.

On the stroke of midnight, there came the *pat-pat-pat* of tiny feet on the floorboards. The robber elves were back! Oddkin and Bodkin had sold every pair of shoes at market, and they had come for more. Again they said these magic words:

Shoes in twos, so fine and neat
SHRINK to fit wee fairy feet!

As before, the shoes shrank to fairy size, and the robbers stole them away.

The next morning Mr Boot overslept. He jumped out of bed at ten o'clock, and ran downstairs to the shop. But, when he saw that he had been robbed again, the shoemaker sat down and cried. And his customers, seeing no shoes for a second day, *tut-tutted* and went away.

"I'm a ruined man!" said Mr Boot.

The unfortunate shoemaker *did* seem well and truly down on his uppers. He had just enough leather to make two pairs of boots. Wearily he cut out the leather and shaped the heels. As he worked, he wished his luck would change for the better.

No sooner had the wish entered his head when an extraordinary thing happened. A rainbow filled the room and a fairy appeared! She was a beautiful fairy, with hair as bright as moonlight, and eyes that twinkled like stars.

65

The shoemaker, who had
been hammering a nail, was so
astonished he missed the nail
and hit his thumb instead.
"*Ouch!*" he cried.
" I'm sorry I startled you," said the fairy.
"I've come about your wish."
So Mr Boot told the fairy about the stolen
shoes. When he had finished she said,
"Put the last two pairs of boots in the
window tonight. We'll watch and see
who comes to steal them."
So the shoemaker
finished the boots, polished
them till he could see his
face in the toes, and left
them in the shop.
Sure enough, as the clock
was striking twelve, Oddkin
and Bodkin came sneaking
in. Mr Boot and the fairy saw
that the elves were dressed in
leather jerkins and breeches.

Oddkin and Bodkin had
bare feet. Although they were
a bit disappointed to find only
two pairs of boots, they decided
to take these for themselves.
"Fine boots!" said Oddkin.
"The very best!" agreed Bodkin.
Then they said these magic words:

Boots for us, so fine and neat
SHRINK to make our dress complete!

Straightaway the boots shrank to just the
right size, and the elves pulled them on. But
before they could run away, the fairy appeared
and cast a spell on the boots. She waved her
magic wand and said,

Shiny boots, so fine and neat,
March those elves right off their feet!

The fairy's
magical powers
were stronger than elf
magic, so the boots obeyed
at once. They marched the elves out
of the shop, at a cracking pace.

"Best foot forward," said the fairy.
"Left, right, left, right!"

"Hey! What's happening?" said Oddkin.

"Stop!" cried Bodkin. "Please, stop!"

But the boots did no such thing. They
marched those robbers to the back of
beyond which, as I'm sure you know, is a
very long way away.

THE BACK OF BEYOND

1,000,000,000 MILES

Mr Boot was as pleased as anything to see them go, and he thanked the fairy for her help. However, the worrying fact remained that since his last two pairs of boots had just walked off, he had nothing left to sell. He didn't wish to appear ungrateful to the fairy, but he tactfully mentioned this problem to her.

"Quite so," said the fairy, who was a bit forgetful. She looked at the shoemaker and saw he was wearing a large leather apron.

She simply tapped the apron with her wand, said some magic words and . . . *POOF!* The apron turned into a pile of shoe leather neatly cut, shaped and ready to sew. Mr Boot was delighted. He had enough leather to make a shop full of shoes for his customers and an extra-special pair for the fairy - the tiniest, weeniest little shoes imaginable.

As for those robber elves, who knows? They could be marching still!

1,000,000,000 MILES

That was a good story, Trip.
If those bad elves
ever come here, I'll tell
them to hop off!

What was that, Pod? You have found my wand? Where? Oh, there behind a pile of pearls. But look, it's bent. Bent!

Will the wand still work, you ask? Well, there is only one way to find out. I shall cast a spell. Let me see . . . some glittery stardust would add a lively touch to the dress, don't you think? I'll just say some magic words,

A sprinkle of stardust in blue, green and pink
To twinkle and sparkle in less than a wink!

and wave my little wand **Ping!**

Deary me, that wasn't quite what I had in mind. That's because the wand is crooked, you see. It's made the magic go wrong. And what's done is done. Spells can't be unpicked as easily as stitches - not with a wonky wand. You wait till I catch Thimble and Thread! I'm sure those two took it when I wasn't looking.

Now we must get on. Time is ticking by and we have two hundred more pearls to sew. Which leaves just enough time to hear one more fairy tale from Nightwing - it's your turn at last. Afterwards it will be time for us to go to the Midsummer Ball!

So, Nightwing, tell us your tale while we're stitching . . .

71

ONE PUMPKIN, FIVE DEARS AND THREE GOOD WISHES

Once upon a time, there was a kind man called Mr Dear. He lived with his wife and their two children in a pumpkin. It was a bit of a squash, but they were happy and content.

Then one sad day the children's mother died, and they all missed her terribly. In time Mr Dear met a lady - quite a large one actually. She smiled a lot, and Mr Dear *thought* she would make a good stepmother for his children. So he asked the lady to marry him, and she agreed.

But the day after they were married, I happened to be passing the pumpkin when I overheard the children's stepmother complaining to their father.

"This pumpkin is much too small for a family," she was saying. "Besides, it's very cold and damp. I wish we lived in a proper little house in the country, with a back door and a front door, an upstairs and a downstairs; and there should be a warm fire to toast my toes by. That's what I wish. So I do!"

It didn't seem much to ask, but Mr Dear was poor. He had nothing in the world except a good kind heart.

"I cannot afford a proper little house, my love, my dearest," he said. "I only wish I could give you what you deserve."

I felt sorry for them. Wouldn't you feel the same for a family all squashed up in a pumpkin? So I went inside, waved my wand and said,

"Your wish will come true. But first you must put your shoes on the wrong feet. Then turn round three times for the magic to begin."

Well, you never saw a family change their shoes so quick. Left feet in right shoes. Right shoes on left feet. All in a hurry.

"Now," said Mrs Dear, wobbling a little on her chubby legs, "we must turn round three times, just like the fairy said."

And they did. No sooner had the Dears stopped turning when the pumpkin turned into a proper little house, with a back door *and* a front door. It was perched on a hill, with countryside round about.

Straightaway the children raced upstairs, ran into all the pretty bedrooms, and bounced on the beds. Meanwhile their stepmother made herself comfortable downstairs, in a big armchair by the fire.

"It's just what you deserve," Mr Dear told his new wife.

I could tell Mrs Dear was pleased (although I did not hear her say Thank You), so I flew away.

Not long afterwards I popped back to see how they were getting on. It was a windy day and the children were flying their kites. They looked very happy, but their stepmother did not.

"This house won't do at all," she was complaining to her husband. "It's much too windy on top of this hill. I have to walk down it to the shops - and all the way up again! I wish we lived in a town house, close by the market. I should have a maid to do the shopping, and all the housework. That's what I wish. So I do!"

"I cannot afford a town house with a maid, my love, my dearest," said Mr Dear. "I only wish I could give you what you deserve."

You can imagine how disappointed I was to hear all this. I thought Mrs Dear would have been satisfied. But I just shrugged my wings, waved my wand and said,

"Your wish will come true. But first you must put your shoes on the wrong feet. Then turn round three times for the magic to begin."

So Mr Dear called his children in from play, and their stepmother told them to put their shoes on the right way (that is, the *wrong* way) again. The children didn't do it quite so quickly this time, because they really didn't want to leave the little house on the hill. But Mr Dear said it was what their stepmother deserved, so put like that no one felt they could argue. When they were ready, they all turned round three times.

I am proud to say my magic worked perfectly for the second time. When the Dears stopped turning, the little house on the hill vanished, and a big house in the middle of a town appeared. It had four floors and an attic; each room was full of fine furniture. Down the street was the busy market - so close you could hear the stallholders shouting. Best of all (Mrs Dear thought) was the maid. She was already busy with a mop and broom.

"It's just what you deserve," Mr Dear told his wife.

Mrs Dear looked happy (although I did not hear her say Thank You) and the children were talking to some new friends next door. So I flew off.

A few weeks later I went back to see if all was well. But oh, no! I heard Mrs Dear grumbling to her husband, worse than ever.

"It's my birthday next Tuesday," she was saying. "I want to have a Big Party, and invite the most important people in the town. This house is much too small for such a special occasion. I wish we lived in a mansion, with a ballroom to dance in, and servants to cook and clean. I should like wardrobes of beautiful clothes, so I should look quite splendid. *That's* what I wish, SO I DO!"

Mr Dear sighed wearily. Even he was getting fed up with his wife's outrageous demands. But because he had a good kind heart he said,

"I cannot afford a mansion with servants, my love, my dearest. I only wish I could give you what you deserve."

I could hardly believe my ears. I had tried my best to please her! But I decided to help for a third time (after all, it *was* her birthday) so I waved my wand and said,

"Your wish will come true. But first you must put your shoes on the wrong feet. Then turn round three times for the magic to begin."

By now the little Dears were good at putting on their shoes the wrong way. Only this time they did it even more slowly because they didn't want to leave their new friends behind. But their stepmother just stamped her foot (not easy when you have your shoes on the wrong feet) and told them to hurry up.

Mr Dear could see how upset his children were. So he whispered in their ears, and told them their friends could come to the mansion as often as they liked. Which cheered them up a bit. After that they all turned round three times and . . .landed in the most magnificent house, with marble pillars and winding stairs. There was a ballroom the size of a football pitch; and wardrobes (too many to count) bursting with dresses - all size 'Extra Large'.

Mr Dear sat down. He was quite overcome by the grandness of it all. He told his wife shakily,

"It is just what you deserve, my love, my dearest."

Soon the children were playing at sliding across the ballroom floor, while Mrs Dear ordered the servants about at the top of her voice. At last I thought she would be happy (although I did not hear her say Thank You). So I went away.

On Tuesday I went to wish Mrs Dear a Happy Birthday - even though she had forgotten to invite me to her party. And do you know what? As soon as she saw me, she complained to me most bitterly.

"The chandeliers in the ballroom are too bright, and they have given me a headache," she said. "The winding staircase makes me giddy and my birthday cake has too much chocolate icing. I feel sick! This isn't what I deserve."

"Oh," I said, waving my wand, "if all you want is what you deserve . . . you shall have it! Just put your shoes on the wrong feet. Then turn round three times for the magic to begin."

Meanwhile Mr Dear and the children were having a lovely time in the ballroom. A band was playing their favourite tunes, so they had all kicked off their shoes to enjoy the dance.

But Mrs Dear couldn't wait to have what she deserved. She hurriedly changed her shoes and spun round three times ALL BY HERSELF. No sooner had she stopped turning when, *poof!* she landed - you'll never guess where - back in the old pumpkin!

When the children heard what had happened to their stepmother they said, "GOOD RIDDANCE!" and carried on dancing.

Mr Dear was a bit upset. After all, he had lost his love, his dearest. But he just sighed and said, "Maybe it is for the best. Now she has *exactly* what she deserves."

From that day on he lived happily with his children. The mansion was very comfortable - they couldn't have wished for anything better. As for the lady in the pumpkin . . . it won't surprise you to know that she complains about it every day. Some people are *very* hard to please. But three good wishes are enough for anyone so . . . in the pumpkin SHE MUST STAY!

Look at the time! Ten ticks to midnight already.
How time flies when we're enjoying fairy stories.

But there's no time for any more tonight. Nightwing, Fancy, Trip and Pod – we must get ready for the Midsummer Ball!

You will come, won't you? Please do. It will be such fun. Every fairy will be there in their finest gowns, masks and dancing shoes. There'll be glow-worms to light the way, and fairy fiddlers to play our favourite tunes till dawn.

And the feast! I cannot tell you how many delicious things there will be to eat – enough to burst your poppers off, I can tell you.

If we can tempt you to come to the ball, **YOU** will be our special guest. We'll even arrange for you to sit next to the Fairy Queen! Yes, really. She will be so pleased to meet you when er, . . . we have made you a little smaller. You won't mind shrinking, will you? Just for one night. It's not the least bit painful and you'll grow again by morning.

You would like to come but you have nothing to wear, did you say? Nonsense! Just close your eyes and wish! Think of something enchanting to put on, and you shall have it. Dressing in Fairyland is as easy as winking, and takes no time at all. So, shut your eyes and **WISH** . . .

Twists and stitches! I can hear the royal trumpets. The Queen is coming! She'll be here in a blink. Pod, pass me a pearl. Just **ONE MORE** - then it's done. There! What do you think? A work of art, don't you agree? You'll never see another dress quite like it.

What was that? Why didn't we make it by magic? Goodness, don't you know? We should never have had time to tell all those stories, you see. Magic is far too quick. Although, now I come to look at it properly . . . I had better wish for another.

There! Isn't that a dream of a dress? And in the nick of time too. The queen is here.

Good evening, Your Majesty! Blossom, Nightwing, Fancy, Trip and Pod - Royal Dressmakers at your service. Please allow us to assist you. And when you are ready, we'll go to the Midsummer Ball!

THE END